I0716637

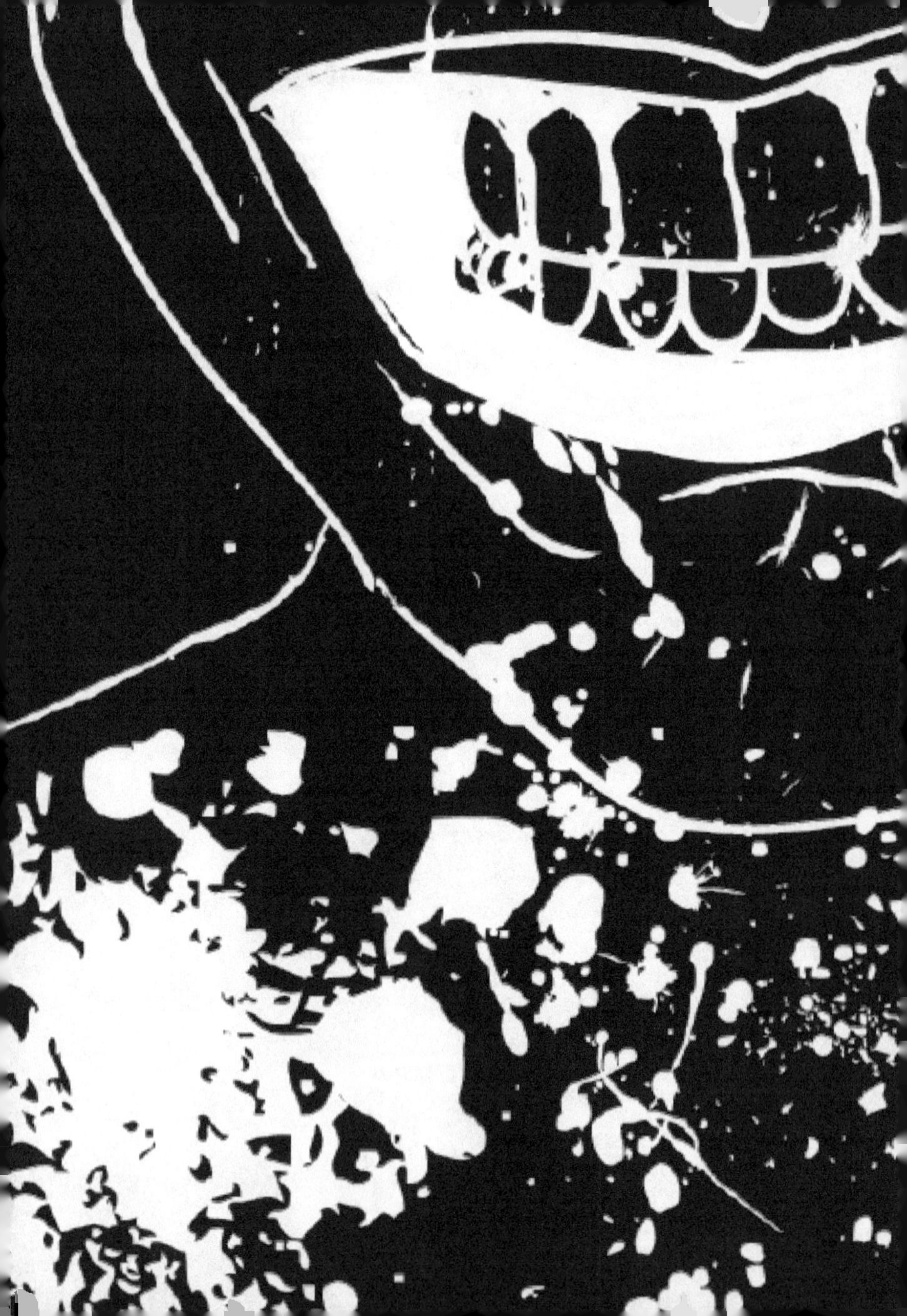

Saturn

Saturn

Stories

Simon Jacobs

Long Day Press
Chicago

Also by Simon Jacobs:

Palaces
Masterworks
String Follow

**This edition is for June,
nascent Bowie fan**

Published by Long Day Press
Chicago, Il 60647
LongDayPress.com

ISBN 978-1-950987-48-1 (Paperback Edition)
ISBN 979-8-8693-4704-6 (eBook Edition)
Library of Congress Control Number: 2024937945

Cover and Layout by Joshua Bohnsack
Illustrations by Andrew Shuta

Previous editions published by Spork Press.

Early versions of several of these pieces appeared in *Handsome, Everyday Genius, Hobart, The Doctor T. J. Eckleburg Review, Spork,* and *Skydeer Helpking*.

Printed in the United States of America.
First Long Day Press Edition

PROUD MEMBER

David Bowie Bids on a Piece of Modern British Art

This is mostly what he does nowadays. It looks, he thinks, like a self-portrait he himself might have painted in the mid-90s with a contemporarily novel blend of acrylic impasto and computer collage (around the time he was also experimenting with interactive CD-ROM technology). This is mostly the reason he buys it.

He hangs the painting in a conspicuous spot in his two-story Soho penthouse. Everyone who sees it, they ask the same thing, "Is this one of yours?" Even his young daughter Lexi, his son, BAFTA-winning filmmaker Duncan Jones, and his wife, Somali supermodel Iman (for whom he has written songs), they all ask: "Is this one of yours?"

"No," David Bowie says. "I haven't painted that way in years," he says. He brings them to his studio and shows them his latest work, a series of classically-styled triptychs inspired by the films of Fritz Lang that in reality draw more from Francis Bacon than Hieronymus Bosch. "See?" he says. "*See?*"

Though they all nod intently, David Bowie fears that they

do not see, and these days when he sings for close friends or family the vibrato in his voice is out of control.

And then, eventually, there comes a certain point when he stops denying it altogether, when people ask about the painting on the wall and David Bowie answers, "Yes. It's one of mine. It has always been one of mine." There comes a time when he stops measuring the distinctions between them, when the colors darken and smear into the background, the brow slopes down the forehead, the left pupil dilates, and it becomes just another picture of him.

David Bowie Watches His Own Cameo in a David Lynch Movie

He admires the Southern accent of his character, Agent Phillip Jeffries, who appears in the film raving about what he's seen only to quite literally disappear two minutes later. His performance reads to him now like pulling it off. David Bowie remembers them, the two Davids, talking like they were brothers about transcendental meditation and Francis Bacon's *Head* paintings (they are approximately the same age). He reflects on an iconic, forty-plus-year musical career that even the most jaded critic wouldn't hesitate to call "classic."

Later, in bed that night, he practices his Southern accent—now over twenty years dormant—on his wife, Somali supermodel Iman (for whom he has written songs). He moans, "Keep Judy outta this!" into her shoulder. She says not bad, "for an Englishman," in a voice drawn across other continents.

David Bowie watches his own cameo
in a David Lynch movie

David Bowie Examines Francisco Goya's *Black Paintings* Shortly After a Massive Heart Attack

Here, the aged artist's fear of insanity, a misanthropy in fourteen paintings, a wash of black and ochre. David Bowie contemplates the waning years of the old deaf Spanish master, spent in a house of paranoia and torment, a house of silence.

He briefly transposes the Quinta del Sordo (whose walls these paintings once covered) with his apartment in Manhattan, where his young daughter Lexi, barely four years old, and his wife, Somali supermodel Iman (for whom he has written songs) wait for him to return; the isolated acreage on Little Tonshi Mountain, purchased last year, where he hasn't started building yet.

David Bowie notes the bulging white eyes of *Saturn Devouring His Son*, the manic hunger of old age. Elsewhere, Atropos prepares to cut the thread of life, and two ghoulish women leer at a man masturbating, a private life breached and cast into stagelight. His touring days are over.

He recalls the distant nights spent in Haddon Hall, the Victorian mansion in Beckenham where he conceived Ziggy

Stardust and his son—aspiring filmmaker Duncan—with his first wife, Angie, nights suffused with drugs and wanton sex, new young bodies that had nothing to lose. Now, a history of pinched nerves—his last performance in Scheeßel, Germany, earlier in 2004, and the collapse backstage; the final encore, the artery that did him in.

David Bowie puts his hands over his ears, shuts his eyes and screams or pretends to scream until the entire gallery is empty. Receptions are only warm for dying stars. He feels a familiar pain in his shoulder. Thrusting his chin upwards—like Goya's *The Dog*, a face of despair mostly buried in the muddy tide, snout uplifted to the dirty sky, always ochre—David Bowie falls to the Museo floor. Old superstitions awaken, and he travels home by boat.

David Bowie Sleeps with *1001 Arabian Nights* Next to His Bed

He reads from it a few pages each night, an ornate, garishly-illustrated 19th-century edition he won in an auction at Sotheby's. It is a premise he recognizes from somewhere: the Sultan, who takes a new bride every night only to murder her in the morning, and Scheherazade, the talespinner who keeps herself alive day after day with a forever expanding mythology, serial reinvention.

Nearly nine years after the massive heart attack that effectively ended his live career, and each gilt page he turns fills David Bowie with dread: he expects the Sultan to kill her, to tire of her guises, her artifice and her costumes—as all singular things are killed on restless nights, thousands upon thousands of them in a desert song.

(4,000 miles away, the Victoria and Albert Museum has opened a retrospective exhibition of his stage outfits and ephemera.)

He turns to his wife of over twenty years, Somali supermodel Iman (for whom he has written songs), and asks her to tell him a story that never ends, in a language he doesn't understand. As she speaks, he traces the tattoo on her stomach with his finger, a ring of script he cannot read that she promises is his first name—David, a name she tells him cannot be properly articulated in the Arabic alphabet. He whispers, "Open, sesame," into her skin, but she covers his mouth with her hand, and he swallows it. David Bowie wonders if Scheherazade ever lost herself among the frayed ends of her legends. He is concerned for the way these sagas end.

David Bowie Attends the Premiere of His Son's Latest Film

For a brief moment, they inhabit the same coast. In the film, Jake Gyllenhaal is forced to repeatedly re-live the last eight minutes in the life of a random stranger on a Chicago-bound train, attempting to prevent the bombing that kills everyone aboard. Its themes are as familiar to David Bowie as breathing, as family, and as they stand facing each other upon the stairs outside the theatre, he recalls other origins: on the birth of his daughter, Lexi, now on the cusp of her teenage years, the doctor told David Bowie that it appeared as though he'd "given her his entire gene pool." Likewise, the resemblance between him and his son, BAFTA-winning filmmaker Duncan Jones, has always been uncanny, and looking at him now it is difficult to see anything other than a younger version of himself, a version without children.

David Bowie feels something welling up inside of him, the terror of one who looks so much like his past. They embrace—while camera flashes surround them—and suddenly his voice sounds hollow. He speaks into his eyes, but all at once David Bowie is relating in nothing but esoteric clichés, in lines he wrote forty years ago: "Don't believe in yourself," he intones, "Knowledge comes with death's release"—lines that have always been about potential.

He laughed. He shook his hand.

When the photos are developed, however, upon further inspection it will appear as though father and son aren't actually touching, but orbiting each other a hair's breadth apart. Looking even closer, it will start to seem as if David Bowie isn't there at all.

David Bowie Watches the Storm Through the Window of His Two-Story Soho Penthouse

In the gale outside, he sees apparitions of the past, faces he's synthesized over the years: the flaming red Ziggy Stardust mullet, the fascist-chic of the Thin White Duke, images from other eras he spent functioning in myth; now, he finds himself slipping inexorably, apocalyptically back into it, for the first time in a decade.

He has just finished recording.

David Bowie thinks back to one of his most infectious melodies, 1972's "Starman" (which foretold a different landing), and, in the chorus, the octaval leap he stole from Judy Garland. They both sang about skies, although his is a different cyclone, the kind with names of women born in the first half of the last century—Dorothy, Sandy—names that would seem petite if not for the wake left by the crook of their final letter.

His wife, Somali supermodel Iman (for whom he has written songs, on other albums), born in another decade, appears just behind him, her face reflected in the glass against his own and the rain, her past slotting in among the others.

In the fog accumulated on the window, Iman writes her name in Arabic. As her finger drags through the perspiration—right to left, against history, against Western sense—a lightning flash illuminates the studio, and superimposed on the glass David Bowie sees behind him a host of faces—his own, his self-portraits, as they have been all along—and suddenly in the glass, her finger curves around its final consonant and he can no longer tell what's past or present.

She touches his shoulder. Water swelling in the street below, they retreat to the bedroom—his family, or what he's localized of them: his wife, Iman, and twelve-year-old daughter, Lexi. David Bowie gathers them together. He thinks of his wife's name trickling down the window. Inside, he names a private storm.

Later, when the city is finally put to sea, David Bowie wonders if the swiftness of its sinking is due to the combined weight of so many icons buried in a single tract of land. Or, their opposites: from the bodies hanging in the sky, spiraling and pulling back. Once again, he is thinking about planets.

David Bowie watches the storm
through the window of his
two-story Soho penthouse

David Bowie and Damien Hirst Collaborate to Build a Minotaur

At last: construction of the labyrinth is underway on one of Greece's uninhabited islands. David Bowie is charged with finding the human donor; Damien Hirst and his assistants are handling the bull head. As he begins his search, David Bowie is amazed and unnerved by how many young people are willing to lay down their lives for him, for Damien Hirst. For both of them. The plan is to graft the two together, the bull head and the donor, to house them in the labryinth.

He more than admires Hirst's work, his spin paintings and dead animals floating in tanks of formaldehyde (although David Bowie feels like he's clearly been given the harder job). He sees the beauty in taking something you love and preserving it forever. He thinks of his wife, Somali supermodel Iman (for whom he has written songs), who lately has thrown herself even more completely into charity work; his son from another marriage, BAFTA-winning filmmaker Duncan Jones, over forty; and his daughter, little Lexi (forever little, though she is creeping towards her teens), who will never stop growing. He imagines them suspended in blue.

David Bowie can't sleep, wrestling with his selection from the art students who eagerly offer themselves to his project. He worries that perhaps Damien Hirst—Britain's richest living artist—uses the word "beautiful" too often when titling his work. David Bowie considers the version of the beast that appeared so prominently in his 1995 concept album *1. Outside*, the first in a planned-but-abandoned album cycle of art and murder in the new millennium, now many years too late— the Minotaur as artist, as murderer. David Bowie is wearing earrings for the first time in twenty years, and the only reason he can tell why is nostalgia.

Three feet below the surface, at the center of a maze on an island off the coast of Crete, David Bowie digs up a priceless, diamond-encrusted skull—one of Hirst's. He realizes, then, that this was never a collaboration at all, but something in-finitely more sinister. He imagines Damien Hirst somewhere else, laughing and laughing.

From then on, David Bowie finds only diamond skulls, heads without bodies.

David Bowie Approaches Tilda Swinton to Play Him in the Movie of His Life

Years ago, he watched her sleeping or feigning sleep inside a glass case at the Serpentine Gallery in London, where she lay eight hours a day for a week, a quiet spectacle of performance. He knelt by the case, peered in at her tranquil expression—like he knew she wasn't faking—and imagined his own, a vulnerability in public repose. He carried the same features, this image with him for nearly twenty long years. David Bowie tells her this.

She pretends a certain energy, as if she'd known he was there watching her in the box, as if, when they'd first worked together—when she appeared opposite him, playing his wife in the video for 2013's "The Stars (Are Out Tonight)"—she hadn't been slowly transforming already. David Bowie tells Tilda Swinton that seeing her now feels like he is the one finally waking up, that it brings him no shame to admit this, despite his teenage daughter Lexi who waits patiently for him back home, a wife—Somali supermodel Iman (for whom he has written songs)—whom he publicly credits with restoring his equilibrium, his love at first sight. Looking into her eyes, David Bowie knows he has made the right decision. He's never noticed it before, but hers are exactly like his.

She tells him she's been preparing for this role her whole life, that she's been watching and studying; in her performance as Orlando, Virginia Woolf's androgynous protagonist who vows to never grow old and awakes halfway through to find themself transformed into a woman, she channeled David Bowie's spirit, she tells him. She agrees to take the part.

They return to their respective homes, the trumpets pealing truth. That night, Iman's husband feels unfamiliar to her: the way he carries himself across the bedroom, the way his feet hit the floor, his weight in the bed. A weird, Northern lilt in his voice, an angular face in the moonlight. A contract is sealed.

David Bowie Builds the House on Little Tonshi Mountain

Architecturally, it is almost an exact replica of the Indonesian-style villa he had constructed on the Caribbean island of Mustique in the late 80s; the original, with its layered streams and koi ponds, Javanese furniture, and rampant teak, barely fit anyone's definition of a house—more than anything, it resembled a palace.

The sixty-four acres of wooded land they call the Mountain—a wild, secluded area upstate, near Woodstock, originally purchased in 2003—has lain dormant for ten years. Earlier than that, he recorded 2002's *Heathen* in these mountains; beneath stark, unforgiving vistas he composed an album of overwhelming spiritual despair, an album born of fear for the world he'd just brought a new child into—his daughter, Lexi, who has just turned thirteen. He builds the house in secret. He watches the same vistas.

When construction is finally complete and the house totally furnished, David Bowie takes Lexi and his wife, Somali supermodel Iman (for whom he has written songs) on a long drive out of the city, into the mountains. David Bowie can barely conceal his excitement; he has them wear blindfolds, and they listen to Richard Strauss's *Last Four Songs* for the whole drive—composed when the master was 84, they're about universality, and death—some of the most romantic music he's ever heard.

Inside the gate, when he has his family remove their blindfolds, Lexi shrieks with delight—she has never seen the original, even—and David Bowie beams. Leading them around the horseshoe-shaped veranda, he shows them the fully-stocked koi ponds, the 19th-century British-retreat living room, the octagonal Javanese guest pavilion, and the curving balustrade that surrounds it all, carved in the shape of the Nāga, the snake-like Hindu deity that carries the elixir of immortality.

Lexi—who has grown up entirely in the city—goes crazy for the deer, and chases them into the sunset by the pool. David Bowie uses the opportunity to give Iman a more intimate tour of the house. Every corner they turn, he acts surprised—a sharp intake of breath, a quick step backwards—as if he's seeing each room for the first time, although it has been built to his precise specifications, although it resembles the house on Mustique in almost every way. At the end of the hallway, he instructs Iman to close her eyes again. "David, I've already seen all of this," she says.

With a flourish, he unveils to her the Egyptian Revival master bedroom. He draws the curtains open, revealing yet another impossible vista, into which they watch their daughter, chasing something invisible, vanish completely. David Bowie imagines his wife draped luxuriously across the bed, her pose reminiscent of a portrait by Rossetti, while he sits a few feet away, painting her.

"Is it all exactly the same?" Iman asks.

David Bowie takes her by the hand with a surprising firmness, and for a second the house no longer feels like an echo, but a part of something frightening and new. "Not exactly," he says, pushing open the door to the observatory. "Not exactly."

David Bowie Takes a Commercial Space Flight

It has taken over fifty years to reach this point. When David Bowie hears the countdown in his headset, each number hits him like a cold bullet and brings him a step closer to 1969, to his first hit, to the inside joke that made him a star. Later, as they're unraveled into orbit—the sixty-minute spacewalk for which he's paid almost everything—David Bowie turns slowly in the less-than-gravity to face his wife, Somali supermodel Iman (for whom he has written songs, unlike this one), only to find that in her spacesuit and helmet she has lost virtually all form.

A voice crackles through his headset, "I love you, Dave," but it is a voice he doesn't recognize. He reaches out and touches her shoulder through six layers of Gore-Tex, nylon, and Mylar. The sensation is like pressing into a fossil.

The line revisits him long after he could be expected to respond: he sings, "Tell my wife I love her very much. She knows." But beyond its topicality and obvious self-reference, Iman knows the truth, just as she knows exactly when her husband was lost to the distant past, and as they unspool from each other David Bowie looks down at the glowing surface beneath them and realizes his mistake: Planet Earth is blue. And white. And green. And yellow. When he returns home he will begin painting again. Somewhere over Tucson, Arizona, a star falls from the sky.

David Bowie takes
a commercial space flight

David Bowie Returns from the War Memorial: Rochester, New York, March 1976

He looks from the road to the passenger seat, to his friend and protégé James Osterberg, Jr., a little less skeletal now than the hospital bed at UCLA where he found him a year before; Jim's best album—1973's unhinged *Raw Power*, on which David Bowie served as producer—lies behind him along a checkered path to recovery, while David Bowie's pools out in front at the same rate as his widening pupils, as the floodlights on his stage.

Jim's outline is lit up at intervals by the flickering lights around the car, turning him into something else as if by photographic manipulation, his body pressed onto a conducting plate and blasted with high voltage, leaving just its aura behind, a corona like a saint's, like the holy son. David Bowie, too, feels changed in a way that he can't yet fully describe, touched by something imminently martyr-like or messianic, a legacy without a fully-formed center. Their collaboration seems fated to continue.

The road to Rochester is paved with the same white

lines as the road to Ypsilanti, to Kether, their skylines equally indistinct and hazing away. On Jim's next album, their roles change in proportion, and the famous mug shot, taken in the usual manner after they're booked that night, absent its Kirlian fields, is David Bowie in everything but name.

David Bowie tracks with bloodshot eyes from his passenger to his own knuckles, spired white across the steering wheel like the cracked turrets of Hunger City, which he invented alone, which has nothing to do with this tour. The moon buzzes as if carbonated. He mixes the backing vocals way, way up.

David Bowie Watches Seminal Massachusetts Hardcore Band Last Lights and Reflects on Nebuchadnezzar's Dream

Another long drive, and a complex series of maneuvers for the 61-year-old legend to stand, unremarked upon, in the corner of a basement venue in Worcester, Massachusetts on an icy night in 2008, hidden beneath many layers. He has grown fond of these clandestine voyages, in the four years since his heart attack, his little excursions outside of the public eye: later, he would find the band for *Blackstar* the same way. Other patrons take him for the progenitor of this venue, perhaps, if they clock his age at all, the man who has seen through every young upstart band to take this stage. Who has been in that same spot, unmoving, nodding along, since whenever the club was founded.

The singer, a red-blonde boy in his early twenties, the microphone cord wrapped around his throat, wields the anxious bravado and physicality of Ian Curtis: sure enough, on his shirt are the wobbly mountains of Joy Division's rotating neutron star. That baritone voice—mimicking, in some respects, Bowie's own—that David Bowie has outlived: Curtis a suicide at 23. It wasn't supposed to happen that way. He was not supposed to outlive his followers.

Something in the scene—the screamed lyrics documenting the rotting carcass of life on Earth; the way the bare stage lights illuminate the strangled singer's hair, turning it golden—calls to his mind the vision of the Prophet Daniel recounting Nebuchadnezzar's dream, which Willem Dafoe's Jesus shares with David Bowie's Pontius Pilate in 1988's *The Last Temptation of Christ*: Daniel described a towering statue with a head of gold, silver shoulders, a bronze stomach, legs of iron, and feet of clay. A stone was thrown and the clay feet broke, and so the statue collapsed. "God threw the stone," says Jesus: "The stone is me."

"And Rome is the statue," David Bowie as Pontius Pilate replied, his South London accent fully intact. The dream foretelling a cascading wave of kingdoms collapsing into one another, like bloody dominos.

This boy is the stone, David Bowie thinks now. He is the stone. Punk rock is the stone. The kids moshing by the stage are the stone. The zines for pay-what-you-want on the table to his left, staffed by no one, are the stone. The gathered energy here, in its collective raw force, is the stone. At one time, David Bowie thinks, he might have been the stone himself. But it is not for him now.

$\star$

After the show, he emerges from the sweltering basement and the midnight December air freezes the sweat on his skin. The next day, following the long drive back to New York, David Bowie checks the Massachusetts hardcore band's MySpace page and learns that the singer has died of a brain aneurysm following the show last night, at age 24. The microphone cord around his neck creating a blood clot that surged to his brain. Another dead kid with too much potential while he sits here, unending, in front of a screen. *A martyr*, he thinks grandly of the singer: a stone cast at the clay feet of the great statue. The great statue of capitalism, of patriarchalism and colonialism and white supremacy and all.

He looks up from his laptop across the living room of his two-story Soho penthouse, from the kitchen island where he sits to the windows overlooking Lafayette Ave: his cone of vision takes in almost $2 million worth of art, post-modern furniture, books, decor, and architectural design, not including the value of the apartment itself.

On the central column hangs his much-discussed 1807 painting by Tintoretto, acquired in 1987, his first major art purchase, an altarpiece of St. Catherine visited by an angel. In the sky hangs the great spiked wheel on which Catherine would be hung, divinely destroyed when she touched it. She rebuked the Roman Empire, over and over, until she was beheaded. *She was the stone.* Now, she is pinned on his wall, a part of his legendary collection.

His trappings laid before him, David Bowie realizes that no, not only is he not the stone: he has become the statue.

He feels his feet quicken, as if sinking into mud. How much of it was necessary, when he was gone? How much to support Iman's beauty empire, to provide for Lexi and her children's children's children? To fund Duncan's next film? To take what remained of his family to the next planet once the earth died? His albums would sell forever. His head, falling to his hands, as heavy as—

"Wake up, brother!" a voice cries in his head, the voice of a flaming red-haired boy who had once rendered himself an alien to liberate humanity from its otherness, and had, likewise, annihilated himself on-stage in front of his bandmates, at the end of being young.

"The writing's on the wall and the apocalypse is at your window! Your treasury is barely worth its weight in rent when the gods are consolidating!" calls the voice. Except it comes in a Boston accent. "Wake up, you sleepyhead!" cries another prodigal son, sucked back into the void.

The living room clarifies before him: a museum. A cathedral. A great jeweled tomb. And he is awake. David Bowie is more awake than he has ever been.

David Bowie Celebrates His Daughter's Birthday on the Anniversary of the Release of His Chart-Topping Single, "Life on Mars?"

Of all the planets, this has proven to be the most commercially successful. In the 1973 video for the track, belatedly released after its parent album (1971's *Hunky Dory*) to capitalize on the mania for Ziggy Stardust, David Bowie appeared dressed in a turquoise Freddie Buretti suit, his face nearly bleached-out against the empty white backdrop but for the flaming red hair and Pierre Laroche makeup, the blue about his mismatched eyes. Together, the composition resembled nothing so much as bright fields of color on a canvas, a pop-art mask of the planet once said to hold life.

On the record sleeve, captured mid-mime, he wore a gold astral sphere painted on his forehead, the area from which, in a different mythology, other planets made their daughters.

But for his own, David Bowie remembers the hospital and the voice of his wife, Somali supermodel Iman (for whom he has written songs), the tight weave of their hands, and then, the birth of his only daughter, Lexi, now into her teens. He remembers it all, so clearly.

(In a January 2013 interview with *The Times* preceding the release of his comeback album, *The Next Day*, longtime collaborator, producer and friend Tony Visconti appointed himself David Bowie's "voice on Earth," implying that, already, he had gone.)

Above her crib: a mobile of the planets, and he stood behind it, staring down at the legends we create.

David Bowie Watches Himself Age 200 Years

In the face of his character, John Blaylock, he witnesses an inescapable conclusion. During the film's sole memorable sequence, David Bowie, playing a vampire, suddenly finds himself aging rapidly, despite the youthful immortality he's enjoyed for the last two centuries. Over the course of a few minutes, his face furrows and sags, his hair falls out in patches, his posture stoops, and his voice drops to a whisper. In the end, his lover, a 6,000-year-old eternal beauty, confines him to a coffin in the attic among the other has-beens, immobile yet undying.

Released in 1983 at the zenith of the most commercially successful album and tour of his career—*Let's Dance* and Serious Moonlight, respectively—*The Hunger* found David Bowie at his physical peak. Today, the film is an omen. He watches himself stab a young girl in the neck. He licks the blood off his fingers. He turns to his wife, Somali supermodel Iman (for whom he has written songs), who sits next to him on the couch with her legs folded beneath her, her flawless skin alight in the glow of the screen. Though she is now well over fifty, David Bowie is struck with the realization that she looks exactly the same as the day they met nearly twenty-five years ago, that while he sits and grows old hourly, she, Iman, has simply, abruptly and entirely, stopped.

David Bowie Attends a Charity Event Hosted by His Wife

There is an auction. This time, he buys a mid-sized African head, something that looks nothing like him, in a technique (late eighteenth-century Maasai) and medium (hand-carved wood) that he has barely touched. This time, there will be no mistake, he thinks, not in this piece, this pre-modern, pre-British piece. In his zeal for its acquisition, he pays too much, but the cost is charitable.

That night, as the foreign statue watches over them in the master bedroom of his two-story Soho penthouse, Iman turns to David Bowie in the dark and asks him why he surrounds himself in his videos with people who look just like him. She asks—harshly, he feels—if he is intent on spending the rest of his career remolding the faces of a past he's promised time and time again to leave behind. Except she uses the word "myths."

David Bowie brings the African head statue to his defense—he points to the technique (late eighteenth-century Maasai) and medium (hand-carved wood), neither of which have anything to do with him; he tells her that he meant for

44

the statue to recall nothing but itself and its own tradition. He reminds her desperately of the songs he's written for her, of the music he composed for their wedding ceremony (much of which was later adapted for inclusion on his 1993 album *Black Tie White Noise*).

But Iman chooses to recall just the one: the shuffling, syncopated wash of Eastern-influenced electronics that bears her last name, Abdulmajid—a track originally recorded during her husband's Berlin period (long before he met her) but only released in 1991 under a new name, hers. She imagines a career, spiraling horribly in on itself, whose ultimate goal is substitution.

All at once, there in the dark of the bedroom the Maasai statue begins to reveal itself: the mismatched eyes; a lightning bolt bisecting its face; a tuft of shocking red hair crowning the scalp—the vengeful god, the red god. A realization floods over her: they can fill their home with whatever they want, but—she hears him singing quietly beside her—their fear is as old as the world.

The next morning David Bowie awakes to find the apartment empty of anyone else. Meanwhile, the Maasai statue has turned to chrome, its technique and medium suddenly, terribly familiar. On the base, a scratched signature reads "*Bo '95*," which, if he'd been listening, he, too, would have recognized as one of his own.

David Bowie Dreams of Taking the Eucharist and Then Wakes up Alone

Despite his religious skepticism, in the dream the ritual felt completely earnest; still, he awakes in a sweat borne of fear. The thought of it, this public sacrament, drives him back to 1992, and the Freddie Mercury Tribute Concert at Wembley Stadium, when he'd knelt down in front of a televised audience of a billion and recited the Lord's Prayer for a friend on another continent, for the victims of a disease worse than time. Four days later, he married his wife, Somali supermodel Iman (for whom he has written songs, yet who is absent from the bed beside him). Nights like these, whenever he confuses the two—his wife with the prayer, his communion with fate—he thinks of the inevitable, introspective melancholy of his 1999 album '*Hours…*', his last of the millennium, released five years before the massive heart attack that brought his touring days to a vicious close.

On the sleeve, a long-haired David Bowie cradles his goateed, short-haired past self like the *Pietà*, the body before the resurrection. It is a different century now, and perhaps this

46

is what terrifies him most: something like eternal return, in which the past rises to consume the present in a never-ending cycle (his career has been built on reinvention)—the finality and unchangeability of everything, even as it circles back. David Bowie scrambles for a poignant lyric but all he can think is "Ashes to Ashes," an epitaph for the wrong decade, and as he realizes he is doomed to live a 21st-century man a metallic taste rises to fill his mouth; not the wine, nor blood, but a precursor to much worse. And so it goes—he reaches again for the wife who isn't there—from station to station, "this is the way the old men ride: hobbledy, hobbledy, hobbledy, down into the ditch."

David Bowie in a Boschian Nightmare

Pale life teems around him, joined together in every configuration, a perversion of the natural order. Nude forms spring fully-grown from enormous, erotic fruits—like gods, he thinks—only to double back and begin feasting on the same. Human limbs sprout from egg-like vessels, one or the other in the midst of ingestion, birth, or reproduction—it is a world of animate flesh captured in transformation, populated by a humanity with no father, no past, only present, blooming and glistening, all one in the same, all bodies. And David Bowie has never been so goddamn hungry.

In this nightmare: God, a skeletal, white-eyed figure in the background, his features oddly familiar, presides over the scene as a ghost might, knowing his hands could no longer touch, could mold nothing. An iconic, nearly fifty-year artistic career and David Bowie has become the "elder statesman" of rock, an old man left to passively herald in the new as his voice goes reedy. (*The New York Times*, citing "Death, the Great Uninventor," called *The Next Day* a "twilight masterpiece"; the implications were clear.)

Elsewhere, in the third of the triptych reserved for hellish torment, the bird-headed devil sits upon a golden throne, swallowing humans whole, only to immediately excrete them undigested into the ground. Beyond, giant ears trample through the blackened wasteland as humanity receives its final comeuppance and cities burn into the sky. It is a nightmare of unbridled appetite, an utter loss of control. Yet when David Bowie opens his mouth to sing, it's the most dangerous, open-throated and honest he's ever sounded in his life.

David Bowie in a Baconian Nightmare

He can no longer tell his screaming face from the background.

David Bowie and the Feasts

It helps to explain the hunger inside of him. He looks at medieval paintings, Renaissance paintings, surrealist paintings; the masters. He pores through the glossy pages of books accumulated over an iconic, fifty-year artistic career spanning virtually every form of media and always ravenous for more, for images of consumption, something hard and hungry at its core: feasts of all kinds—sexual, religious, mythological.

David Bowie searches, from Rousseau's lion throwing itself on an antelope, to the Boschian feast at Cana—where no one is eating anything—to the revelry of Rubens's Venus, to Pieter Bruegel's peasants and their gruel. (This reminds him, of course, of Bruegel's painting *Landscape with the Fall of Icarus*, which has gnawed at him for years and was so crucial to the 1976 film *The Man Who Fell to Earth*, in which David Bowie, as always, inhabited the role of the otherworldly outsider. In the much-lauded painting, country life goes obliviously about its business as Icarus drowns off the coast.)

Images roiling in his head, David Bowie decides to make

a painting of his own, a portrait of his wife of nearly twenty-five years, Somali supermodel Iman (for whom he has written songs), from a photo of her posing like an Egon Schiele model. But when he finishes, there is something missing: a gauntness to her face, her skin sallow, hair falling lank onto her knobby shoulders; emptied of something vital, it's the worst she's looked in her entire life.

David Bowie sees none of this. It's the eyes where the painting loses its faithfulness, he thinks. Always, always the eyes, like those of Rousseau's lion, vicious but strangely passive, staring blankly forward like two mismatched black voids filled with something desperate. They are his eyes.

David Bowie Confronts His Digital Self in *Omikron: the Nomad Soul*

This, too, is something he recovers from the 90s. David Bowie is amazed by his likeness in the game: in addition to contributing an album's worth of music to the soundtrack, he plays Boz, the leader of a shadowy anti-government movement called "The Awakened." David Bowie hears his own voice, watches a rendered face motion-captured over fifteen years ago, telling him: "The survival of your soul is at stake." He recalls how he was initially attracted to this project by its distinctly Buddhist undertones; how, when you die in the game, you're reincarnated into the body of whatever character is nearest, whoever touched you last.

With the skyline of Omikron in his screen and that of lower Manhattan in the window, David Bowie plays for hours, leaping from body to body. He searches for his next and only reincarnation, his wife, Somali supermodel Iman (for whom he has written songs)—who has a cameo in the game, same as him—but who, across four million rearranging pixels of color, is nowhere to be found. Over two decades of history between them, and for some reason David Bowie cannot remember the last time they held hands, whether or not it was her he touched last.

On the street below: the skeletal mendicant with the milky eyes, whose features remind him of something he's seen in a painting, the old roué who always grabs his shoulder as he walks past, beckons through the night for David Bowie to follow, to follow. "Was she never there? Was she ever?" David Bowie asks himself, and this, too, is a quote, although suddenly, for the life of him, he can't remember from where.

David Bowie Devouring His Son

And the image falls across him like a fever: what distinguishes him from Goya's painting of Saturn is the eyes, wide and terrified, the left pupil permanently dilated from a childhood fight with a boy whose father never had the courage to do as he does now. David Bowie feels his massive hands gripping the bloody husk of a body before him, its head and left arm already consumed, a sinuous trail from mouth to shoulder, his giant white knuckles and thumbs touching on either side. (The body seems tiny—he thinks this must be part of being a god, the smallness of ordinary things.)

To this, David Bowie compares the body he once held each night, that of his wife, Somali supermodel Iman (for whom he has written songs): its ungainly limbs, the tangy flavor; the BAFTA-winning film career, the happily married but childless life, all the potential he's ended.

David Bowie recalls his schizophrenic half-brother Terry (whose suicide he bravely confronted in 1993's "Jump They Say"), and the others who haunted the wards of Cane Hill, those he would have once called madmen. He remembers a line recorded in 1970 but written even earlier—he sings it, through his mouthful: "God's a young man too." The album on which it appeared, *The Man Who Sold the World*, depicts him (in a composition derived from Rossetti), wavy hair down to his shoulders, reclined on a chaise longue in a satin, cream-and-blue Michael Fish dress, cards scattered all over the floor like he had any license to play with fate—you can buy God, or you can be him.

These, in any case, will be the myths we feed our children. It's here, David Bowie thinks, in this portrait, of the cannibal aesthete and the cannibal god, in the planet dominant on the day he was born almost seventy years ago: a legacy all his own, the undeniable, incontrovertible proof that he never, he never lost control.

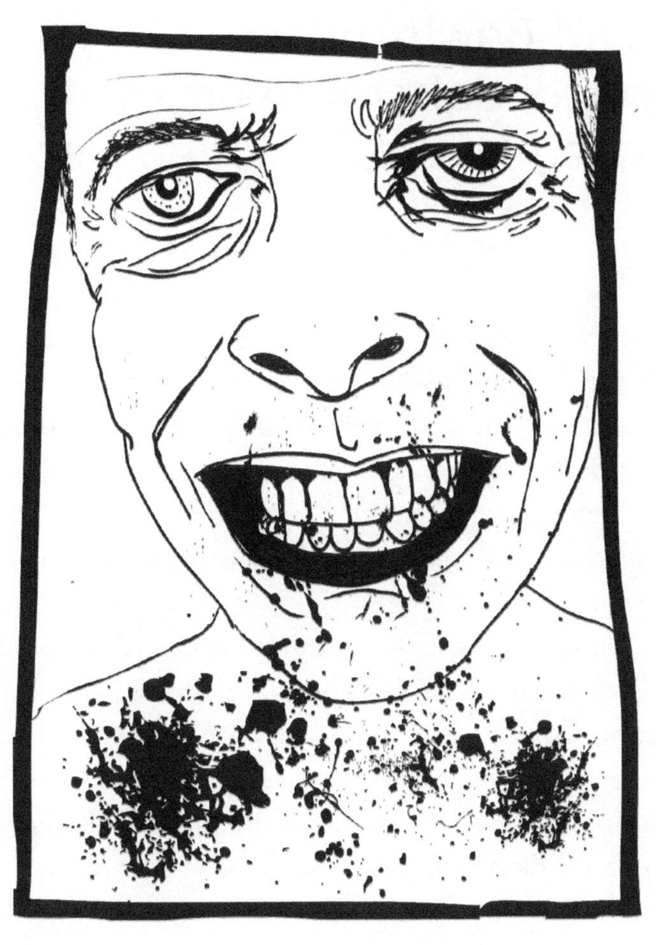

David Bowie devouring his son

David Bowie Takes Ryuichi Sakamoto on a Long-Overdue Coffee Date

They have to spend some time catching up about the 80s, and their first and only collaboration in 1983's *Merry Christmas Mr. Lawrence*, with David Bowie as Major Jack Celliers, a British POW, and Ryuichi Sakamoto (who also composed the score) as Captain Yonoi, the repressed commandant of the internment camp—the two stars at the respective pinnacles of their global fame.

The soaking heat of the Cook Islands standing in for Japan-occupied Java. Nagisa Oshima, the laconic auteur director, draped in mosquito netting, who rarely left his chair, waving away multiple takes. Bowie ends the movie buried up to his neck in punishment for his insolence, left in the sun to bake and die a curly bleach-blonde saint, the same hair he wore for the Serious Moonlight tour to support *Let's Dance* the following year.

It was the healthiest David Bowie had looked in years, on that tour (the most commercially successful of his career)—a proper superstar's twenty-trailer caravan, his cocaine habit down to afterparty levels. On the album cover, he was shirtless and muscular, in boxing gloves, the victor over his demons: it was only because David Bowie felt so wholly healthy that he could lean so hard into playing a wastrel. The first acting gig he'd treated like a *role*, rather than an extension of himself.

Now, thirty years later, a dozen international tours between them, the silver-haired icons sit at a discreet cafe in the West Village within walking distance from each of their homes, the two so comfortably settled over decades into their germane urban celebrity that they almost consider sitting outside, because the weather is so nice.

They reflect on their month in the South Pacific: the isolated set meant they spent most evenings together, David Bowie gliding across the hotel pool in the moonlight, positively basking in his exercise regimen, while Ryuichi Sakamoto reclined in a rattan deck chair, shaded in palm fronds, soaking in the ambient buzz of the night. He had an affected pair of sunglasses he wore all the time off-set. Ryuichi Sakamoto remembered a kid, no more than thirteen and speaking no English or Japanese, who repeatedly sprang from the bushes to offer him drinks at all hours of the night, wherever he was on the hotel grounds. Bowie six years his senior, a meteor: what was ever going through his head? "Two musicians learning to be actors," Ryuichi Sakamoto says now, in the West Village cafe. It hurts to speak, a little.

"Learning to be human again, really," says David Bowie, sipping green tea. "The seventies were monstrous."

Ryuichi Sakamoto smiles. "Of course, we are both now old men, and all too human."

A faint clatter of a cup or silverware striking a wooden table, elsewhere in the cafe. David Bowie absently touches his side, near the lump beneath his rib cage, a lump that has not ceased growing. He catches Ryuichi Sakamoto's eyes as if to ask, *Yours?*

Ryuichi Sakamoto puts a hand to the base of his neck in a gesture of equal deference. *The throat.* He shrugs. "But I was never much of a singer."

David Bowie smiles mischievously. "Ah, but neither was I." And the heaviness evaporates. They swap stories of their recent treatments, progress and setbacks: a snapshot of where they're at. To their mutual surprise they find they share a dietitian. A jasmine plant in her office that for some reason makes David Bowie vomit when he smells it. The receptionist relocates it now, before he goes in. Though he might not go back in again, since just thinking about it makes him nauseous. But what kind of reason is that to stop seeing someone?

"We never talked about music either, back then." Ryuichi Sakamoto laughs, eventually.

"No, we didn't. Funnily enough. I suppose I was very focused on being an actor."

"I was in awe of you," Ryuichi Sakamoto says.

"And I was in awe of myself," he dodges.

At a lull in the conversation, they notice at around the same time the ambient soundtrack of the cafe, a drippy acoustic cover of "La vie en rose." Tiring of metaphor, Ryuichi Sakamoto stands and suggests they go for a walk. "I wish they would let me choose the music," he says. "I despise this. It causes me anguish."

They walk the four blocks to the park, briskly, side by side, in companionable silence. A purposeful walk David Bowie has mastered, sunglasses and hat on, to keep strangers from stopping him in the street. Neither walks like a sick man.

When they arrive, the park is deserted, as bare as a stage. There is not a soul around. Who could say when the rote sounds of the city faded away? David Bowie looks back at where they entered, and while he can see people passing on the sidewalk, the figures look as though they are a world away, separated by an intangible barrier, like shadows on a cave wall.

A grand piano sits empty in an inlet of the park. Ryuichi Sakamoto looks around for its owner, and seeing no one, he sits down on the bench. He puts his phone atop the piano. *It would be a waste...* He flexes his fingers and plays a few notes, then a few more: a water-light trickle he has just improvised, which drifts off into the air as if summoning rain.

"I could never stop composing, though," Ryuichi

Sakamoto had said, back at the cafe. "It was like my blood, always pumping."

For reasons he cannot articulate, David Bowie lays down on the ground, beside the piano. He stares up into the flat, white sky, bisected by the underside of the piano, a row of dark wood slats. The sun shifts behind a cloud, provoking a spear of light. A drop of rain dews the corner of his eye.

Above him, Ryuichi Sakamoto plays. The muffled, thumping ring of the keys reminds him of the clicks from an MRI machine, sending their weird signals through the walls. The melody rematerializing from rain to fog, and back again.

An intake of breath, in and out, resounds in the cavernous wooden space beneath the piano. The smell of beech trees fills his nostrils as David Bowie inhales. The trace of a vocal line returns to him at last.

David Bowie and
the Shining City

At the beginning of the century, he named his daughter. As always, it was a pastiche of ancient cultures and distant shores: Alexandria for the Ptolemaic library; Zahra, the Arabic word for "flower," for "luminous," the name of the palace-city in medieval Spain; and Jones, the surname David Bowie left behind long ago, a name synonymous with anonymity, because Bowie had always been plastic to begin with.

Earlier that year, Iman gave him a book of translated Andalusi poetry for their anniversary, and it was from here that they drew the middle name, from Ibn Zaydūn's yearning, elegiac ode "Written from al-Zahra," which conflates the ruins of the so-called "shining city"—the effective capital of 10th-century Muslim Spain, sacked early in the 11th by civil war, and long known for its elaborate gardens and towering architecture, its overwhelming majesty—with a long-lost lover, finding her features in the beautiful and tarnished landscape.

In the classical Arabic original, Iman told him, the lover is mutable and collective, substituting the history of a displaced people, a fallen region for the lovelorn narrator. The English translation westernizes the poem, turns it into yet another sonnet about a girl, as basic as anything. Ibn Zaydūn, she said, had broader intentions than simple fusion. He knew that the luminosity of the city was drawn from its shadow, was heightened by distance.

Fifteen years later, his own star at his shoulder, David Bowie records his final album. Simultaneously, he begins production work on his co-written musical *Lazarus* at the New York Theatre Workshop, a successor to *The Man Who Fell to Earth*—the role he originated in 1976—incorporating his back catalogue. It is as close to a retrospective as the great reinventor is willing to get.

There is joy in these months, and David Bowie works furiously: he feels the familiar thrill of collaboration—with Tony Visconti, his producer stretching forty years; with the jazz band he'd enlisted for *Blackstar* after seeing them perform in Greenwich Village; with the cast of Lazarus—the creative burst that comes with recording new material and rearranging old, from charging these instincts. He enjoys the daily circuit from his Manhattan apartment to the Magic Shop to the NYTW, the city where he moves namelessly through the crowd (his home now for twenty years), this narrow orbit and the familiar gravity of his family: his wife Iman, his daughter Lexi, now fifteen, and his son Duncan, returned to the city to finish postproduction on his new film. He pulls them close and holds them there at the core. The dreams end—they all do.

David Bowie composes the new album with arcana, with the knowledge he has accumulated over his lifetime, oblique references to his past and future—the harmonica from 1977's "A New Career in a New Town," the diamond-encrusted skull, a lexicon borrowed from Burgess (dormant since he toured as Ziggy Stardust), Elvis. He pulls each strand down from the stars like books off a familiar shelf. He feels that he has the entire universe to pick from.

The weather cools as autumn passes, but barely. His pace accelerates.

He studies afresh the work of Joseph Turner, the Romantic painter. These days, David Bowie prefers the later works, when the artist abandoned typical patterns of composition and began painting from some interior architecture built of pure light and sea foam, when the storms seemed to wreck the very canvases they were painted on (never one for posterity, Turner painted with materials that suited his purpose at the time, regardless of how they would age, frantic in his ceaseless creation). David Bowie reads about the Year Without a Summer in 1816, a year of global drought brought on by a volcanic eruption in modern-day Indonesia, during which the ash in the atmosphere produced the intense, unearthly sunsets from which Turner drew his inspiration. Turner's stock in trade, late in life, was in pitting nature against man, and showing how man always lost. He always lost.

A thousand years after Ibn Zaydūn, five hundred after the fall of Granada and the onset of the Inquisition, Mahmoud Darwish composed his own ode to the leavings of al-Andalus, and again it stood for something else, was a symbol of resurrection in which—once one was separated from the physical plane—all that was left behind was a tower of memory and manuscripts; with the bricks, other towers were built, other cities. "Was Andalusia here or there?" he wrote, "On the land… or in the poem?" The cities go on forever.

At the start of the new year, winter finally arrives. Each sunset is more brilliant than the one before it.

In the last photo published of him, David Bowie looks spry and indomitable, poised as if for launch, beaming beneath a wide-brimmed hat reminiscent of his days on the set of *The Man Who Fell to Earth*, an object recovered without history or malice, the way one pouts for the camera draped in a thrift store feather boa, liberated from the burden of its past, the separate life of its former owner.

And fitting: in the closing scene of *Lazarus*, Thomas Jerome Newton (now played by Michael C. Hall, inheriting the mantle from David Bowie), after languishing on our planet for something like seventy years—the reign of al-Zahra, the time it takes for a legend to crystallize—at last releases the ties that bind him to this culture, this Earth, and finally (symbolically, at least) returns to the stars.

Publicity for the new album reaches its pitch—it's his best since *Scary Monsters*, as always—and the world braces once again for his reappearance, his name on everyone's lips. Inside, David Bowie recalls Turner's famous, reputed last words, whispered from Turner's adopted house in Cheyne Walk overlooking the Thames, where he'd lived under an assumed name for almost twenty years: "The Sun is God."

And he rises to greet the dawn.

Acknowledgments

I wrote the first story of *Saturn* in 2011. The book was first published by Spork Press in 2014, and then in an expanded edition in 2016, two months after David Bowie died. This is the first edition to be bound by machines, and I am forever grateful to Spork for their finely wrought care for this project over the years.

Thank you to Drew Burk, Andrew Shuta, Joel Smith, Richard Siken, and the generations of Spork interns and accomplices that brought this book to life—at least twice. And thank you to Josh Bohnsack for bringing it to life yet again, and allowing me to revisit it. This edition includes two new stories, and minor edits to a handful of existing stories.

Thank you to Sam, Junebug, and my parents and brothers.

Thank you to Chelsea Hodson, and the Morning Writing Club.

Thank you to David Bowie, without whom I would be quite different.

—Simon Jacobs
Portland, OR
December 2023

Simon Jacobs is the author of the novels *String Follow* (MCD/FSG) and *Palaces* (Two Dollar Radio), and two collections of short fiction: *Masterworks* (Instar Books), and *Saturn* (Long Day Press). He is from Dayton, Ohio, and lives in Portland, Oregon with his family.

Long Day Press

New & Forthcoming Titles

G a i n e s v i l l e
Colin   Winnette
N   o   v   e   l
ISBN: 9781950987474   • $16

We   Go   Liquid
Christian   TeBordo
N   o   v   e   l
ISBN: 9781950987412   • $16

An   Atavic   Fear   of   Hailstorms
João   Reis
N   o   v   e   l   l   a
ISBN: 9781950987290   • $14

Girl   Thing
Morghen   Tidd
S   t   o   r   i   e   s
ISBN: 9781950987368   • $16

LongDayPress.com   @LongDayPress